Narratives In Monochrome

"Narratives in Monochrome"

ISBN No: " 978-93-91302-27-6"
1st Edition
Language – English and Hindi

Flairs and Glairs
Publication House
Regd. Under MSME Act.

Disclaimer

This is a work of fiction and solely represent the thoughts of the corresponding authors of the articles. Our editors have tried their best to edit the content of all the authors and check the plagiarism.
All the write-ups in this book are unique and are only published in this book.
In case any plagiarism or error is found, only the author is responsible alone, and not the publisher or the Compilers.

Cover Designing and Book Formatting
Shubham Shah and Ishani Agarwal

Co-Authors

Shubham Shah (Founder Flairs and Glairs)
Ishani Agarwal (Co-Founder Flairs and Glairs)
Rashmi Pai-Prabhu (Compiler and Editor)

1. Author Urvashi Tandon
2. Author Abhishek Kumar Anmol
3. Author Vedant Sharma
4. Author Abhishek Kumar Shandilya
5. Author Anubhav Bakshi
6 Author Soutam Banerjee
7 Author Jhimli Parui
8 Author Rohit Verma
9 Author Kiran Hiwale
10. Author Eswar Bodduri
11. Author Gautam
12. Author Lavnya Krishnamurthy
13. Author Hiranya Verma
14. Author Rakesh Deshpande
15. Author Noufer Aboobacker
16. Author Aayush Das
17. Author Fouz
18. Author Abhijeet Kumar
19. Author Achal Mogla
20. Author Kavitha Arjun
21. Author Nitin Sharma
22. Author Jeena R Papaadi
23. Author Jihan K Patel
24. Author Namit
25. Author Vineet Ahlawat
26. Author Sripremraj
27. Author Shaiwal

28. Author Sandeep Bogra
29. Author Rashmi Chand
30. Author Bilal K Shaikh
31. Author Ananyaa Salve
32. Author Saurav Ranjan Datta
33. Author Shilpa Salve
34. Author Rima Sen
35. Author Vijayalatha. N
36. Author Aysha Latheef
37. Author Anika Gulati
38. Author Amal Hassan
39. Author Mohit Sharma
40. Author Vivek Dutta Mishra

Shubham Shah

(Founder- Flairs and Glairs)

Shubham Shah, an entrepreneur at "Flairs & Glairs" a brand with dynamics in events organizing and cultural educational pan INDIA, is a 26yrs old guy who recently has entered the digital platform of imprinting emotions. He has initiated with his own open mic platform to help budding poets and aspiring writers under his brand named as "Teekhe Zasbaaat"

He is a commerce graduate from the Bhagalpur City of Bihar.
He states Writing has impersonated him since childhood and he has now been writing for over a decade!
Cooking, on the other hand, is his passion! He also mentions, trying out new things just tickles him!
When asked sir, Why SPICY EMOTIONS?
He smiled and added, "agar jasbaat teekhe na ho toh wo jasbaat kahan" Spices are all that blends! So do his words!
As a chef, he presents to you his dish! Hot and freshly served! Taste it! Feel it! Enjoy it! You can also find his writing in the Book "Teekhe Zasbaaat" and 50+ Co-authored anthologies. With his passion to explore opportunities across Platforms, he is working with keen devotion and We wish him all the very best for his future ventures.
He is Featured in the International Magazine DeMode for his upcoming solo novel.
He is Approved by Ne8x for its Lit Fest, and is a Golden Star Awards 2020 Winner.
He is a India Book of Records Holder for his Anthology Satrang, and has the Grandmaster title by Asia Book of Records, for the same.
He has also been featured in Prabhat Khabar, Dainik Jagran, and a lot of other Newspapers in Bihar for his achievements.
He has been a proud co-author to
India Book Of Records (Title- Black)
World Book Of Records (Title -15 Wonders of Poetries)
India Book Of Records (Title - Aaina)
Vajra World Records Holder (Title - Gustakhi Maaf Hai)
High Range of Records Holder (Title - Gustakhi Maaf Hai)
Indian Book of Records
(Title - Road from Worst to Best)

Share your reviews on his

INSTAGRAM

@spicy_emotions
@shubham4shah

Or via email on

shubham2shah@gmail.com

To stay tuned to his work and opportunities follow his business Handles

INSTAGRAM FACEBOOK YOUTUBE

@flairsandglairs
@teekhezasbaaat

WEBSITE:

https://flairsandglairs.in/
https://flairsandglairs.com/

Ishani Agarwal

(Co-Founder- Flairs and Glairs)

Ishani Agarwal hails from the City of Joy, Kolkata.
She is the co-founder of her Community "Teekhe Zasbaaat" and Flairs and Glairs Publication.
Been a Compiler for 45+ Anthologies, she is in the process for more. Co-authored in 150+ Anthologies. She is a India Book of Records Holder, a Vajra World Records Holder, a High Range of Records Holder, an OMG Book of Records Holder, a Bravo Record holder, a Forever Star Book of World Records and an Indian Book of Records Holder.
Approved by Ne8x for its Lit Fest 2020, and Literary Icon 2020. Also a Golden Star Awards Winner 2020.
She has also been awarded with India Star Republic Award 2021, a part of She Awards by Awards Arc and Winner of Nari Samman 2021 by Literoma.

She is also selected as Best Achiever of the Year by AwardsArc and Most Challenging Compiler Award by Spectrum Awards.
She got her first solo Published,a solo Compilation consisting of first 750 contents of hers, titled "Hand That Burnt While Healing".

She has been featured by the National Magazine "Taree Zameen Par" with the title 'unstoppable'.
Also featured in the International Magazine DeMode for her upcoming solo novel, she is proud to write on social issues, and is happy with the love she is receiving.
Connect with her on Instagram: @Ishani_agarwal_quotes / @compilations_so_far

RASHMI PAI-PRABHU

Rashmi Pai-Prabhu has a strong penchant for words. The quickest way through her heart is a healthy concoction of 'great language' coupled with 'perfect grammar'. It is hence inevitable that she writes too. Not regularly, but when creativity strikes and apathy subsides.
Fiercely independent by choice, Happy by chance, she is an Architect by education, a Japanese translator by profession and a Writer by passion! She is a mother to an almost 46 year old :) and an almost 15 year old and still struggling to stay afloat!!

Rashmi stays in Bangalore and is a covid-19 survivor who compiled and edited this anthology during her quarantine days.
The following story is somewhat inspired by her personal experience.
She can be reached through her Instagram handle @pai.rash.

COVID-19

Senior Mrs Sinha wiped her sweat on the pallu of her crisp cotton saree and determinedly raced down the stairs. Her other hand clutched a phone in a vice like grip and she continued to sneak furtive glances at it. As she passed Mrs Bose on the landing, she didn't even acknowledge the other lady's warm and friendly greeting and continued swiftly on her way. "How unfriendly was that" decided Mrs Bose, screwing up her already upturned nose.

Hailing an auto-rickshaw just outside her apartment building and whisking out a savlon disinfectant spray from the confines of her tote, Mrs Sinha proceeded to douse its entire interior. "She is so paranoid" thought the fuming auto driver as a visibly tense Mrs Sinha kept fiddling with the phone again while barely mouthing her destination. At the medical store, she seemed preoccupied with the phone yet again; though she took great care to don her gloves before doing the required currency exchange. "Some people, really", laughed the chemist as he put away the currency notes.

At the vegetable store, Mrs Sinha ignored the small talk of the vendor and didn't bargain as she normally would have. The only thing she told the vendor crisply was to wear his mask properly as it had started riding down his nose. The offended vegetable vendor gave her a cold stare but she seemed oblivious and was lost in the phone screen again. Upon arriving back in her apartment building, almost bent double under the weight of all the bags in her hand, Mrs Sinha coldly ignored the lift man's offer to help. "What a snooty old one, of course we wash our hands too" mumbled the lift man under his breath turning away.

Entering home and quickly closing the door behind her, Mrs Sinha breathed a sigh of relief dropping all the heavy bags right by the door. As if on cue, the phone beeped finally indicating a new message. She barely glanced at it and she knew. Mrs Sinha lived alone. She had given her RT-PCR test yesterday and the phone was displaying the result.

Mrs Sinha had been detected as Covid-19 positive and her fifteen day quarantine would start tomorrow. She was all set!

URVASHI TANDON

Urvashi Tandon is a Professor of Anaesthesiology who served the armed forces for 29 years. She is based in Gurugram and has written short stories for anthologies as well as articles for various magazines. She was one of 25 winners of a short story writing contest for women writers of India, held by eShe magazine which culminated in a book titled “Everything Changed After That”. She has authored a book for children titled “Potpourri, stories for children” which is an illustrated book comprising a collection of 10 short stories aimed at increasing environmental awareness in children.

THE SOLITARY TRAVELLER

Dev drove into the motel off the highway. He was tired and hungry as it had been eight hours of driving nonstop. A sandwich and a flask with 3 cups of coffee was all that he had consumed enroute. The blue neon lights seemed so inviting. He sighed as he pulled the hand brake. It was an effort to straighten himself out as he stepped out of the car. Some hot soup is what he needed right away. There was an elderly gentleman at the dimly lit reception, who booked him in. The corridors seemed deserted, but it was just a matter of one night Dev thought. Having ordered his tomato soup and a hearty meal of paratha and chicken masala, he quickly showered and dropped into bed. He was fast asleep when the sound of someone persistently knocking on his door woke him up. He wearily lifted his stiff frame and answered the door. To his surprise and annoyance, there was no one there. Dev cursed under his breath and got into bed again. Just as he was drifting away into the realms of dreams, the sound of the toilet flush being used startled him. That was strange, as he was not sharing the room with anyone. Could it be from a neighbouring room? He decided to check. There was no one in the bathroom but the sound of water filling in the flush tank was distinct. Dev frowned as he headed back to the bed. As he switched on the lights, he noticed an indentation on the pillow where his head had lain but wait, what was this? There was a similar indentation on the pillow beside his!!! Dev sat up in bed with a start! He was drenched in sweat as he tried to calm his racing heart. Thank God it was just a dream but how real it felt. He turned on the bedside lamp to drink some water. The clock showed the hour as 3.45 AM. He decided to catch his forty winks while he still had time as a long road journey was planned for tomorrow as well. The sound of running water from the next room woke him up. He stretched feeling well rested and sat up in bed. As he put on his slippers, he glanced at the other pillow. There was a familiar indentation on it!

ABHISHEK KUMAR ANMOL

Abhishek Kumar Anmol started implementing poetry in the form of nature, justice, crime based on deep lessons given by his mother's soul which vanished early and he learnt how to sustain himself in this world. His book names fossil of time, dawn in the day, an echo of silence mostly describes the leaning towards a new day

GUILT NOT FOUND

This story is about three friends, of silence and of a false message which is a sign that leads to loss of money and friendship. They all are business partners. A crime happens when a single mistake occurs and they are not aware of it. Rohan is a 23 year old boy and the student of an engineering college. Sonu is a 22 year old boy and also the student of an engineering college. Amit 21 year old is a really innocent child who belongs to a high class family. Sonali is a 23 years old shy girl. They all are business partners. It is around 5pm and climate is cool with a pleasant wind blowing. Rohan and Sonu are sitting in their room and waiting for the opening of the stock market. On Monday when Rohan and Sonu ask the 'person' for money, they will be investing it in the stock market. But Amit has been quite sensible and has stopped himself from investing any money in stock market until now. Amit is either not interested in investing or he invests a little amount of money. He sometimes gives a small amount of money and sometimes a large amount to Rohan to invest. Amit always stops Rohan from investing any money in the stock market because he loses a large amount and is aware of it. After one month one day, Sonu calls Amit when the latter is having breakfast and Amit receives the call. Sonu starts asking about investment money but Amit says he has none and drops the call. But an encouraging message is received from a local investor and it is a fake message. After few days Amit invests as per the message and loses all of his money. This is completely planned by Rohan and gang. They have stepped towards a new stage of crime. Rohan and Sonu never admit the whole issue. Money is the big obsession that they have; a terrible psychological and evil plan has been hatched to harm the other person involved. In the end too they never realise about friendship and they only believe in money and nothing else.

VEDANT SHARMA

Vedant sharma lives in agra. He is 10 years of age. He has successfully published his first book in August 2020. Science fiction, dark is his genre

CARNIVAL OF DOOM

Long ago there was a psychotic killer on the loose in 1984 who went by the name of 'Hexagon'. He was on a killing rampage for two years and in the aftermath of it 250 people lost their lives! Fortunately he was caught, got a death sentence and had to leave his wife and his daughter behind! After ten years Hexagon's daughter Celina grew up to be a normal person, but eventually she became a psychopath and opened a mobile carnival, there she would lure people in and kill them for her own enjoyment. Celine and her carnival would stay in a city for thirty days and kill about twenty people and move on to the next city. The C.I.A become very suspicious of that carnival as everywhere it went many people went missing and were later found dead. So they sent out a team of four operatives: Daisy Johnson, Jemma Simmons, Yoyo Rodriguez and Leopold Fitz. Celina then moved her carnival to L.A which was a fatal mistake. The four went into the carnival and they saw a little boy going into a dark room. They sent Daisy in to protect the child. After a while Daisy came running back terrified and said "Guys, I followed my brother into the room and saw him dead!. Jemma replied "You must have imagined it." Daisy claimed "I can show you guys the body." They all went into the room and there was no body but just a head and legs! They were terrified and quickly clicked a picture as evidence but Celina saw it! The squad rushed out of the room but were immediately knocked out by Celina and her psychotic crew. When they woke up they were tied to chairs. Leopold being the doctor of the group used reverse psychology to get an explanation on how Daisy saw her dead brother and after a few minutes they got an explanation. Celina's chemists had developed a gas which seeped into people's mind and created a hallucination of a person they most loved and that's how she lured her victims. The crew managed to free their hands which were tied with only duct tape and attacked Celina and knocked her out. And then everyone heard a voice. They turned and saw their dead loved ones. Meanwhile Celina woke up with a gun pointed at them.

ABHISHEK KUMAR SHANDILYA

Abhishek Kumar Shandilya is a bilingual poet and writer who pens in Hindi and English. He hails from Daudnagar in Aurangabad district of Bihar and currently works as an assistant teacher in English at a convent school in Gaya. Apart from writing poems, he also writes short-stories, novels, musings and quotes. His poems come from the depths of his conscience and are very pleasing to one's heart and mind. This postgraduate writer in English from Magadh University has a sharp mind. His ideas are thrilling and inspiring. Abhishek Kumar Shandilya has very

effectively written poems with beautiful insights on the subject of love and pathos and human emotions. He certainly has the best collection of composition. He has a sharp vision. His initial work was published under the name Origin (the 'beginning)'. He wrote the first novella in English, "Intention". He also translated some Hindi poems which were published by his collection of poems titled Piquant Brook. Abhishek Kumar Shandilya's The Pequent Brook is the first book to be published in English translation of Hindi poetry collection (Awaz bhi deh hai). The scope of his poems may be small but the things contained in them are esoteric.

FIRST LOVE

Those days were filled with romance like other teenagers experience today. He was especially growing fond of one girl named Sarika. She was not pretty yet looked good to him. He used to sit gazing out from his window, and look down the street in the evening. There he sat and stared out across the street upon the building painted white on all its sides. San did not think about anything but the bright-eyed young girl in the window who looked up to the same moon, and thought of her distant home in the city where she came from. One day, she suddenly lifted a kid in her arms. Raising her face, she saw his eyes gazing at her from the next window given the angle of the street. She was a little surprised at first, but in the next moment she started singing a lullaby to the kid. "Do you like it?" she said to the baby looking towards San; then immediately repented that action so much so that her tongue came out from her mouth. "I do," was the answer from his heart which she definitely could not hear, but perhaps must have felt. She took her scarf and began to twist it with embarrassment. "I didn't mean anything," she smiled at last. "I just wanted to know if you are sad." She was speaking to the baby in her lap. He smiled. The smile irked her; he was making fun of her. She disappeared from the spot. San stood a bit longer looking after her, hoping that she would return. Then repenting, he hid his face in his knee, and thought. "Oh, dear, I didn't mean to be angry". The next morning he was up before daylight, and waited for hours with expectation for the curtain of her window to be raised. She greeted him politely; threw a quick glance around the street to see if she was being observed, and then tossed her hair back with style back over her shoulder. As days passed, he found himself frequently glancing at her window in the hope to

find another glimpse of her face, but the curtain remained drawn and Sarika remained invisible .Thinking back at those moments, the memories appeared so clearly that it seemed to have happened just yesterday. Even today, those memories are dear to him and make him smile whenever he feels low.

ANUBHAV BAKSHI

Anubhav Bakshi is the author of spy thriller 'Retribution - The Hunt for a Traitor', and children fantasy book 'Gia And The Old Magician'. He lives in Delhi. He is also a regular blogger. He works for an International Airline and has travelled the world. Through his literary work he intends to create entrancing stories for all age groups.

PARENT TRAP

"They will again be late for school. I have told you countless times that they need to sleep early," said Kabir, looking at the clock. "Kabir! Let them sleep for some more time," replied Nisha. "They need to learn to respect the time. And there is no age for that," retorted Kabir. While they were arguing, Mira, their daughter, woke up and came out of her room and headed to bathroom. After a while Mira went back to her room, where Veer was still fast asleep. "Veer, get up. You know what happens when we get late." "Didi, please let me sleep for some more time," said Veer, trying hard to hold on to his blanket. But Mira applied all her strength and pulled the blanket off. Veer got up angrily, and stormed out of the room. "Veer, Mira, are you ready or not? Breakfast is getting cold; I've made your favorite *Poori-Bhaji*. You will not be able to eat if you are late." The kids' eyes widened and they quickly got ready, and rushed to the dining table. They filled their plates with *poori-bhaji* and started eating. Kabir started smiling. He always loved the sight of his kids enjoying their meal. "Veer, hurry-up, the bus would be here soon," said Mira. Veer quickly wore his shoes, grabbed his school bag and dashed towards the door. Mira followed suit. "Mira, Veer! Aren't you forgetting something? "Mira and Veer turned around and ran to where Kabir and Nisha were standing. They folded their hands, and bowed their heads. Kabir and Nisha smiled and waved kisses at them. Then the kids got up and ran out. Just as they were exiting, Mira turned and said, "Thanks Granny." And Veer shouted from a distance, "And thanks for the yummy breakfast Granny." Granny shut the door and turned around. There was a picture of Kabir and Nisha on the wall. It had been three years since their untimely death in an accident. Granny looked at the

picture, and then wiped a tear off her cheek. "You left too soon. These kids need you." Kabir and Nisha, still standing under their picture, looked at her, and then looked at each other. A faint smile erupted at their lips. "We never left. We will always be with them," both said, as their figures slowly faded from the scene.

SOUTAM BANERJEE

Born in the City of Joy in the early 90s, Soutam Banerjee has been working with the country's largest steel producer since the last five years. He is involved in the quality control and inspection of rails, wheels and axles for Indian Railways, something on which the entire nation moves forward. A nerd with a vibrant smile for the outer world and an ardent admirer of reel life love stories, his overflowing emotions are confined to his pillows only. Just like an average Indian kid, he spent his growing up years mostly by mugging up his textbooks. Alas, he stayed aloof from the rich and diversified world of literature. Loads of

insignificant lectures and some indispensable friendships, his college years added nothing significant beyond this to his mundane life. A run-of-the-mill job with few plain vanilla aspirations, he was trapped in this vicious circle with everyone pulling him down when he considered diving into the unmapped depths of his life almost a year ago. Being cursed with the act of overthinking, it turns out to be a blessing in disguise when he wishes to pen down his story to vent out his feelings trapped inside since a long time

THE AUTUMN OF EVIL

The season of love and betrayal has arrived once again. When the catkins can be seen bobbing their heads with the wind, it marks the arrival of autumn for me. With Autumn knocking on the door impatiently; love can be seen blooming in a desolated land far away yet so close, colours can be seen cuddling each other on the distressed canvas, hopes can be seen rising from the grave holding on to each other's arms with a promise not to be disheartened anymore, the *shiuli* flowers can be seen reviving life in a dispirited piece of rock, the stars can be seen making grumpy faces when the incompetent clouds try to overshadow them in the clear evening skies, the overburdened leaves can be seen losing their grin when they start discolouring from green to orange to brown, the daylight can be seen losing its lustre with the darkness hovering over it like a nightmare, the winter can be seen smirking at the apocalypse of the mighty Sun's splendid reign and last but not the least, Durga can be seen driving to her homeland from the Himalayas in an old jalopy car with Shiva getting high on weed and her kids in the backseat playing with Ganesha's tummy all along the way.

This year too, the amygdala triggered all these emotions inside me upon its arrival. But, the Autumnal scenes are slightly different this year. The experienced robber came yet again; but this time around a girl's pride was being ruptured far away yet so close, her dignity was being soiled and its remains were buried, the fragile male egos were climbing newer levels to distort her identity, their masculinity was smirking at her broken hymen, the night skies were ashamed as they were incompetent to save her from those demons, the dark nights were crying out loud on listening to her screams and Durga was keen on returning back to Himalayas when she witnessed how real Durgas were being treated in her cursed motherland. The scenes might be devastating and traumatic, but every autumn comes with a shimmer of hope that Good always triumphs over the Evil. No matter how brutal and barbaric the evil deeds are, the good deeds will definitely countervail them by the end just like the Autumnal Equinox.

JHIMLI PARUI

Jhimli is a software professional and working as AVP with a leading UK Bank. She is an Electronics Engineer and an IIMC Alumni. Storytelling and poetry writing has been her hobby since childhood. The Shield Maidens is her first offering which listed in Goodreads and Amazon. She possesses a keen interest in social work as well.
She can be connected via Instagram @jhimli.p

SOLACE OF LOVE

The train departed from Nizamuddin station. Amit was traveling to Ujjain, rather a small town Shajapur which is around an hour away from Ujjain. He was thrilled and excited about his visit. It's been more than a decade now since he last visited Shajapur's Udhaan Orphanage. As the train gained speed, a glimpse of old memories creped in while peeping from his 1st class coupe window. He was fortunate enough to be discovered by wonderful parents who adopted him at the age of 5. Initially, he used to visit once every year to meet his Dai-Maa, Mrs. Ashima Devi the owner of the Orphanage. He had made a promise to Muniya, his partner in crime in the Orphanage. He has now set out to fulfil the same after twelve years. "Will she remember our promise? How does she look like now? Does she still call herself - Muniya?" The questions kept on juggling in his mind. "Sir, Tea or Coffee??" The pantry vendor obtruded into his thoughts. "Okay, one tea with 3 spoons sugar." "One tea with 3 spoons sugar." Another voice echoed from the co-passenger. "You both need 3 spoons sugar?" The vendor was astonished. Amit looked at her. She removed the magazine which was covering the panorama of her face. She had big twinkling eyes, half curly hair, and light pink lips. She hardly had any make-up, yet her face was glowing like the sunshine. She just gave an affectionate smile in answer. Amit introduced himself and inquired about her whereabouts. She mentioned that her name was Anjali. While conversing, Amit found her as a well-known personality who owned three NGOs. It was like love at first sight for him. He felt as if she could have been his Muniya. But he recalled his promise for Muniya to meet her on her 25th Birthday at the Orphanage. Finally, the train reached Ujjain and they bid goodbye to each other.

He reached his Orphanage and met everyone over there. But Muniya was still not there. He went to the peepul tree where they promised to meet. He waited for her till evening but she did not come. He went back to the Orphanage with teary eyes. The wind of solace was blowing on. The peepul tree was the only witness. A train ticket was lying there on the ground - Delhi to Ujjain, 1st class, Anjali Devi.

ROHIT VERMA

Rohit Verma is a Hyperbaric and Diving physician. When he is not at work, he writes a blog, photographs birds, paints absurd watercolours and undertakes long and short trips across the globe. He seeks interesting questions and not their answers as he believes the questions are more important than the answers. He blogs at www.mumbaijamming.blogspot.com and you can see his birds and paintings at @wormholetraveller on Instagram

IN SEARCH OF MASALA DOSA

It's a Sunday morning. The breakfast is cereal. My mind rebels. It craves for something spicy and exotic. Anything but those healthy cereals. I try to find co-conspirators in this rebellion but the family is lazily celebrating the Sunday morning and are loath for any revolutions. I Google the nearest Kamat's, a mere 1.5 km away - a 19 minute walk. I trudge on the dusty pavement encumbered by litter, homeless and dog poop. I dodge the multiple double-parked cars, monstrous BEST buses and the gargantuan construction sites of the Mumbai Metro. These really take away the joy of walking. I reach the Kamat's three minutes faster. It is closed. There is a Cafe Coffee Day but now I am fixated on the Masala Dosa. For a few minutes I stand perplexed. I decide to go to Churchgate. Afterall, whenever in doubt, go to the railway station. All the answers lie there. I take a cab and disembark in front of Eros. Looking for inspiration, I enter Churchgate. Tibbs Frankies? Vada Pao? Wheeler's Bookstall? I exit the station and move to Shiv Sagar. It can barely seat 10 people. All full. The waiter beckons and points to a freshly vacated seat. I share the table with three others who are sipping Mosambi Juices. I order a Masala Dosa and it speedily arrives without fuss. I dig into it greedily, singeing my tongue. Soon I am done with the all but the masala part. I order a plain dosa. Like a domesticated elephant is used to tame a wild one, I consume the masala part with the new and crisp plain dosa. The filter coffee arrives just as I am taming the last bits of the masala. And now I want to leisurely sip on my coffee. The Mosambi Juice drinkers have long left and the seats are empty. The waiter is looking at me impatiently. There is a family of four waiting, looking menacingly at me. Their hungry eyes are imploring me to finish my coffee fast. I

finish my coffee, pay and leave with an uncomfortable feeling of distended stomach. A good brisk walk should help me. I walk to the Flora Fountain and look up the footpath booksellers. 'The lives of Indian Princes' at ₹350. I am in no mood to haggle. I move away and catch a cab back home, the quest for Masala Dosa accomplished.

KIRAN HIWALE

Kiran is an IT professional who mainly writes project plans and reports but indulges in writing short stories and poetry in his free time. His essays were published in a local newspaper during childhood. His stories have been published in two other anthologies. A couple of his poems were published in the digital magazine Unicorn.
He can be reached via his Instagram handle @Kiranh26

THE NIGHTMARE

Rohan was getting ready for office on a dull Monday morning. He quickly took a shower, put on formals, and rushed to the dining table for breakfast.

"I had a nightmare last night," Rohini, his wife, said, "Ride the bike carefully in the traffic."

"What was the nightmare?"

"A truck dashes you while passing by. I don't even want to remember it!" Rohini shrugged.

"Don't take the nightmare too seriously. Our brain just simulates situations that we have heard before," Rohan downplayed the nightmare.

"You still don't believe that I sometimes see the future, right?" Rohini sounded dejected, "One day, you will experience and then believe it!"

"I didn't mean to show disbelief! Don't worry; I will be extra careful today, I promise!" Rohan pinched his neck near his vocal chords as a sign of promise.

Rohini smiled and handed him his lunch box. After Rohan kissed her goodbye, she went to the balcony. Rohan took out his bike. Sachin, who worked in the same company but in a different department, was also ready on his bike. Rohan waved at her, and both men rode out of the society gate.

"Leaving office now!" Rohan texted at 6 pm, and Rohini again became conscious about her nightmare.

"Come back safe!" She texted.

"Yes, dear, don't worry!"

However, Rohini became restless. Her nightmares had come true in the past. She had mentioned it to Rohan multiple times since their marriage about five months ago, but having a scientific mind, he never believed her. On the contrary, he considered it as her attempt to control him through the made-

up stories. A few things happened in his presence, but he brushed those off just as coincidences.

“Oh, God, please take care of him,” Rohini prayed to God. She prepared tea and *upma* for his snacks and waited for him on the balcony. Rohini let a sigh of relief as soon as Rohan entered the society gate. She hugged him tight as he entered home.

“See, I came home safe!”

“I am happy to be proved wrong!” Rohini’s mood cheered up. They had tea and *upma* together while talking about each other’s day.

Suddenly, Rohini’s mobile rang. Strangely, Sarika, Sachin’s wife, was calling her instead of texting.

“Hey, Sarika, what’s up?”

“Has Rohan already returned home? I just got a call from someone that Sachin has met with an accident…”

ESWAR BODDURI

Eswar bodduri is a software engineer from Accenture. He aspires to write more. Previously he published a book 'AM I A BITCH?' and currently working for various Telugu demo films as a dialogue writer.

YOU CAN'T STEP INTO MY SHOE

"No... No...What happened to you? Stupid, leave me, leave me, alone. Why are you kissing me suddenly? Your fingers are trapped in my musty pages and dust has covered your lips. What happened to you coward?" The cover of a book scolds its writer while he was kissing and hugging the book after eight months of its publishing.

"Where are you going without saying anything? Hello boss, I am talking to you, reply to me." The writer gets a cloth to wipe the dust on it.

"Boss, boss this side, here, at the top-right corner." "What happened to him? It's almost eight months since he has picked me, anyhow I am getting cleaned, and that's the happiest thing for me." But, the question is "Why is he doing this? Is he ruining my happiness?" Then I heard the calling bell. The author goes and welcomes a person into the hall. "Congratulations sir, for your best Booker award. I am here to interview you." The man says.

"Whaaaaaaat? I am that valuable? I have gone through myself more than 100 times but never noticed anything special in it. It's a regular dramatic love story. That too this coward of an author has given it a negative ending by parting the lovers." The cover of the book has these thoughts within it though!.

"Thank you!" the writer responds to the person.

"Sir, before going into the interview, I want to ask you one thing out of my curiosity," the interviewer says to the writer. And the writer nods at him.

"Did you ever expect your book to get an award? Sorry to say this, but it's a regular love story, that too with a negative ending."

"Have you ever loved?" The writer asks the interviewer.

"Yes, and we got married too." The interviewer responds to the writer.
"Then, how can you know the beauty of pain." He says this while searching around the room. I don't know what he is looking for but he has turned to me and taken me into his hands. "Like this, for example. This book was printed eight months ago and since then a relationship and a bond has been built up between the cover and the pages in it. If we separate them..." saying this he proceeds to tear me from the book…

GAUTAM

Gautam Choudhury is business analyst by profession and enjoys writing as a hobby. He has published a full length novel earlier and a few short stories. He is fond of reading and traveling. Gautam is active on the social media and can be reached via his Instagram handle @gautam.world.

THE MIRROR

"I will not leave you, Akash. Never." Those were Naira's last words that Akash remembered. They were on a picnic to the hills adjoining the city with their close friends. Akash and Naira knew each other since their childhood. To him, Naira was nothing more than a good friend. He had no idea Naira was in love with him. They had joined the same college where Akash met Anjali, and they started seeing each other without anyone's knowledge. It was at a valentine's party during their last college year when something unexpected happened. Someone announced that Akash and Naira were a couple. Akash vividly remembered Naira's reaction. She started throwing everything around her and left the party in a fit of rage. Naira did not come to college for the next few days. She had blocked all modes of communication with Akash, even refusing to see him when he visited her house. A couple of weeks later, she finally appeared in the college and apologized to Akash and Anjali for her behaviour. Things seemed to have gotten back to normal. Naira was back to her usual self. After their college exams, Naira proposed a picnic to the nearby hills. Their gang of friends joined them. At the picnic, Akash called Naira away and told her he wanted to marry Anjali after college after joining his dad's business. "I will not leave you, Akash. Never." Naira replied. Seeing Akash's baffled expression, Naira broke into laughter. "Oh, Akash. You turned serious. I was joking." "You know, you had gotten me scared," Akash said, finally smiling. "It's alright," Naira smiled back, "But I shall not leave you Akash. Never," she added in a mocking tone. The news came in the next day. Naira had killed herself by slitting her wrists. From then onwards, Akash lived with a pang of guilt. A good three years had passed since the incident. Akash finally got married to Anjali today. He was waiting for her in his suite.

Anjali appeared in a little while in her bridal attire. She looked at Akash and smiled. But suddenly, the smile turned sinister. Akash turned around to see if anyone else was there when his gaze fell on Anjali's reflection in the mirror. It was Naira staring at him in the same bridal dress. "I shall not leave you, Akash. Never," Akash heard. Then everything turned black, followed by Anjali's scream.

LAVNYA KRISHNAMURTHY

Dr. Lavnya Krishnamurthy hails from the pleasant and picturesque city of Coimbatore. She is a doctor (Ophthalmologist) by profession and a writer by passion. She is also an avid reader, foodie and a die-hard Potterhead. She also has to her credit, her first novel *'I Prescribe Love'*, published and released by Leadstart Corporation. She currently resides in Coimbatore, pursuing both her profession and her passion actively.

THE BIRTHDAY GIFT

It should have been the happiest day of her life. After all, who could possibly have their birthday and wedding on the same day? Mahesh lovingly looked at her after tying the *Mangalsutra* and made his promise to be with her forever. The word 'promise' brought an instant, painful recollection of Arjun's parting words to her, two months ago. "It's just a medical camp, I will be back in one week, I promise." In the first two years after their marriage, Mahesh's unconditional love had healed all her wounds. He had become her friend, philosopher and support system, all rolled into one. Three years later, on her twenty-ninth birthday, she sat by her husband, waiting for him to wake up. He had been diagnosed with a rare and aggressive form of lung cancer, three months ago. As warned by his doctor, the cancer had attacked all his organs with a vengeance despite the most powerful chemotherapy. Today he opened his yellowed and sunken eyes as he slowly said to her, "I have a birthday gift for you dear. You can come in now, doctor!" Pushing open the already slightly ajar door, Dr. Arjun came in with hesitant strides. She stood up in utter shock, still not letting go of Mahesh's hand, as her other free hand shot to cover her open mouth. "How…" she finally managed, looking at her dying husband, who continued to have a weak yet goofy smile on his face. "I had a car accident, Ananya, while coming back from the camp that day. A nasty head injury made me lose all my memories. All except…" "He forgot everything except you, Ananya! That was why I found a picture of you in his wallet, when he had accidentally left it behind in the hospital canteen. He profusely thanked me when I returned it. Since then, we became the best of friends!" "And you… you convinced him to…" she said, looking back and forth between her husband and her ex-lover. Mahesh just kept smiling in response. Ananya was now looking at Mahesh, a myriad of emotions playing in her liquid brown eyes. Before he himself or she could cry he quickly said, “Better take good care of my Annu okay doc? Otherwise, I swear I shall come back from the grave to haunt you!” He looked at her smiling face. He then closed his eyes in peace.

HIRANYA VERMA

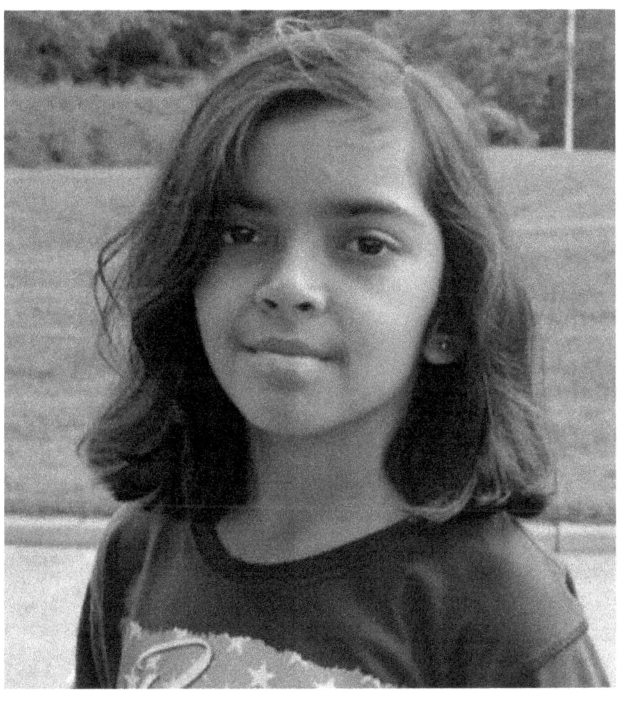

Hiranya Verma is an eleven years old, vivacious, cheerful girl, studying in Standard VII, in Navy Children School, Kochi. She was born at Mumbai on 25 Jun 2009 and her parents are Dr Rohit Verma and Dr Vidhu Bhatnagar. She has an elder sibling, who is three years elder to her and she shares a brilliant equation with her brother Kaustubh. Her hobbies are drawing and painting, reading and writing. She also plays Keyboard and loves the experience called life. She had published her first book 'Hats, Hoods and Humiliation' (Kindle edition) in 2020. When asked about why she chose such a topic to write about, she explained: "I used to think that those movies about high school (the ones with a hero/heroine facing the stereotypical 'popular' evil

girl/boy) were so much different than our real life, especially considering humiliation. It turns out I was wrong. Looking back on my life, I saw that I did get humiliated, more than I thought. I wrote this book because it helped me realize and let go of the shock of knowing and feeling the times I've been humiliated." She has also recently published her second book 'The misadventures and mishaps of poor chap' (kindle edition) which was part of Kindle writing competition. Her third book, a follow up on the first one, titled Ecstatic Eccentric Emotions is under publication.

WHY DID IT HAVE TO END?

It was raining. She could see it outside the window. It wasn't the usual dark, stormy kinds she admired, but a simple shower wasn't so bad either. She decided it was the perfect time to cycle. No raincoat, rain-boots, or even an umbrella. Her *chappals* would do. She zoomed across, feeling the tiny raindrops land on her. The leaves were an altogether different, richer green, and their trunks and branches had on a new shade of brown. The wonderful aroma of wet earth and flourishing greenery reached her nose. She took in a deep breath. This reminded her of the time she took a rainy walk across a tiny miniature city in a foreign country, which reminded her of her trips to foreign countries... No! Memories could come later. She would take in all she could right now, right in this moment, just in case it ended. She left her cycle, thinking it was a great time to play ball instead. She got out her rugged tennis ball, and bounced it around. She threw it up h-i-i-i-g-h, running around to see where it fell. She knew it wasn't a great idea to run on slippery tiles with nothing but *chappals*, but none of that mattered right now. What mattered was the ball. She swung it high, trying to make it reach the branches of a lofty tree. It disappointed her each time, either falling back in a straight line, or in the opposite direction, or just missing the branch. It was great fun, though. She wondered if the kingfisher would come back at this time. But of course, all birds were busy taking shelter under the shade of trees, or sleeping in their nests. The Kingfisher might be abiding in his palace, waiting for the shower to end. She played her little toss-up-the-ball game for a while and then she saw the sun in a distance. She ran towards it, and admired the beautiful sunlight falling on her skin. It seemed so pretty and...beautiful. Suddenly she looked around. The rain had stopped. The only drops which were falling were the dew on the leaves. Oh why, oh why did it have to end?

RAKESH DESHPANDE

Rakesh Deshpande is a passionate writer, and always striving for knowledge. He believes in 'If it's not a happy ending, it isn't an end at all' and aims to develop a positive attitude towards life in people through his writing.

THE EXPECTATIONS

I was walking by the side of the busy road when I received a phone call. Although I was tired, I checked it. It was from an unknown number. As I was rushing to catch a bus back to my hostel, I ignored the call and kept the phone back in my pocket. I couldn't get any seat as the bus was too crowded. In such a peak hour in the evening, getting a comfortable place to stand all the way to my stop was still a blessing for me. And so far, I was blessed three out of ten times. My stop was still one hour away when I felt the phone vibrating in my pocket. I wanted to check if it's her. The love of my life. Although she had called me only when she needed help, I had always stepped forward without hesitation. You shouldn't have any expectations when you are in a relationship else you will be often disappointed. That's what she told me whenever I confronted her. In some way, she had made sense in the beginning. I had thought for several days scrutinizing every point of view. The connection between us was weakening. The affection was slowly fading out. The pain and the disappointment were more frequent than the happiness and the serenity. Although some part of me loved her unconditionally, my self-righteousness wanted to investigate the reasons. I wanted to know if I was the culprit or the victim. I couldn't conclude so far. Now, here I was, following my routine like I did yesterday. The day before yesterday. And the day before that. I got down at my stop and shrugged, freeing myself from irritation. The phone started to vibrate again. It was the interviewer. He had called to inform me that I was selected as an Analyst. It was unexpected but I was excited and uncontrollably happy. I was waiting for almost weeks to hear from them and it finally happened. Then it hit me. Hit me hard. Expectations may hurt but it's natural. There can't be a relationship without expectations. Then I went to her and tried to justify my point. But she was neither attentive nor supportive. In the pursuit of explaining this to her, I found the answer to my quest. I was a victim. A Victim of innocence and loving her unconditionally. Was I not right?

NOUFER ABOOBACKER

Noufer Aboobacker is from a village South Punnayoor Kerala, India currently a resident of Abu Dhabi, U. A. E and an engineer by profession. This International award - winning director is devoted to giving his readers fast paced, high -stakes adventures with stories that are sure to melt their hearts. When he isn't writing you might find Noufer wandering the city with a film camera in his hand.

MIDST OF HUSTLE AND BUSTLE

"Whenever death reaches me please sit by my side for some time" I cannot deny those words that Alice said in my ears long years ago as a joke. That is why despite this busy life, I am travelling from Europe to Asia, just to see her for the last time. Today Alice is the wife of another man and mother of his children, although at one time she was mine. I am trying to accept the truth that I won't be able to see Alice in this life again. A stridulous realization. It's time to say a final goodbye. Alice is now 43 years old. We'd known each other since we were 19. It is fascinating how we only seem to commemorate the good stuff when someone dies. There are several things that I want to say her. I had thought that a day, time and an opportunity will come and she will always be there. But now when she dies those opportunities will die with her. And no one can stop all this. It is natural. As you get older the pace of loss grows faster. Getting old alone and dying is my fear now. I seriously believe that Alice herself will be present at her own funeral invisibly and she will want to see everyone while lying in her coffin. Now what she joked about has come true. When death reaches Alice I will be sitting beside her for the last time. "You came in the midst of all this hustle and bustle?" This may be what she wants to ask me now. She has been inviting me for a long time to visit the place where she lives but it is only today that I will be able to get there. We move on after our losses. But keeping the memory of someone we lost who was an influential part of our life will be intriguing. May all that is left to say remain with me as a memory just like Alice. Now, a child comes forward and holds my hand. It is five year old daughter of Alice. "Uncle! Mom is asleep now. She will get up in a little while and play with me." the child says. Not knowing how to answer that, I stand there stunned. Tears that have not flowed until now fall in front of the innocence of this child.

AAYUSH DAS

Since 1994, Aayush has been an undercover member of the fabled Illuminati. He has a day job, he goes to the gym for about twenty days in one calendar year, and he lives in the most inconspicuous country on the planet. He writes stories and novels about the most unworldly things. Like a true escapist, he is lazy and rarely finishes the books that he starts writing.

THE CHALLENGE

She should've known his intent the moment he took a hit without even trying to block or dodge. John Chadwick's dojo hadn't sprung into existence from nowhere. Aikido had been in his family for three generations before John, and he had inherited combat acumen and dexterity as a legacy. Mei Fang was no rookie either. She was the prodigy who became the youngest black belt in the history of her town twelve years ago. But John Chadwick was different from anyone she had ever fought. When she challenged him, he had simply nodded and taken a stance. His students retreated in a human circle, honouring the ancient tradition of martial arts dojos. The first move was hers to make. A swift kick into the opponent's solar plexus was the perfect way to begin. She quickly followed it with a knee to the temple, taking John completely off balance. She moved in for a grapple to end the fight before the bewildered students could move a muscle. Except, the students were frozen stiff for another reason entirely! Mei was certain of her victory as she pulled her opponent's arm towards her until he said "watch closely" loud enough for the entire hall. His arm moved like butter, but with a little flick freed itself from her grasp. His feet clasped against her hips, tugging her away ever so slightly and then easing off as soon as she resisted. A classic ju-jitsu move. Before she could protest, he had flipped her over his head and sprung upon her. Her hands were trapped behind the small of her back and her opponent's full weight lumbered over her chest, focused through his knee. She was choked for space, for breath, for moves to make. "There you go students", John strained as he announced. "A classic example of an over-eager push resulting in a quick takedown. Remember, always gauge your opponent's strength and tactics before making a move,

not after you've already drawn them and yourselves in the thick of things." "Of course", he continued speaking, "Sensei Mei Fang was just trying to help me demonstrate this to you. The dramatic entrance, though, was my idea. Don't go thinking that an actual fight between me and her would end like this." Mei smiled a little as she relaxed. He was partially correct. A fight between her and John wouldn't end like this again.

'

FOUZ

Fouz is a teacher by profession and a published author. She lives in Kerala. Her first book is a collection of poetry with her drawings named "Dilemmatic" which travels through the different emotions of women. She has also co- authored a poetry book named "Whispers of the Heart".

A CO(VID) EXISTENCE

Shamziya was floating on clouds and was just about to reach the realm of butterflies. *"Damn! That was close!"*

She dismissed the alarm and laughed like an idiot while rewinding the dream. *"Oh! It's court day!"* The sticky note on bathroom door read, "Court at 9.30"

It's been tough 2 years convincing her family about how she survived. An abusive marriage of 13 years! She must live and provide her girls a home filled with liberty, compassion and acceptance. Life of a single mother will be hard but will be worth it.

While running out, her mom called from behind, *"Will the lawyer be there for you?"*

"Yes maa. He will be there on time"

Like a butterfly flapping its baby wings, she rode her scooty. Then the first bus that will take her to city. Side seat view was perfect. Smell of petrichor aroused her nostrils.

At the court standing outside, she saw her lawyer Sandeep sitting in the first row of court room. She waved at him and he waved back. Many names were called out and heard. The court procedures are too novel for her.

After standing there for almost an hour she heard her name being called. She looked at lawyer Sandeep. He gestured her to come forward so the judge can see her. Shamziya smiled politely and awkwardly to the judge. The opposition lawyer was already confronting the judge with a plea to extend the date of hearing as his client (her husband) will be in India on 25th April. She didn't want to hear the rest but figured out that the judge postponed the hearing to April 26th. Petrichor smelt like ashes.

It was mid-March as the country struck with corona virus. The PM announced a complete lock down in the country and boom! To survive was the only mission.

A year passed and no court procedures happened ever since. Shamziya slowly lost faith in the judiciary but her heart already felt the liberty if not in papers.

Not giving up, we are here to stay put. She has learned to be happy being herself, standing on her own feet, paying her bills, pursuing her passion, and what more? Shamziya's girls are proud of her.

"Life is here, happening now, in the middle of human and inhuman viruses. It's what YOU create while unlearning everything that's been taught to you"

ABHIJEET KUMAR

An Engineer and Manager, Abhijeet, holds a post-graduate degree from the Indian Institute of Forest Management. With great love and concern for the environment, he keeps himself engaged mostly in nature and wildlife. His weekends are typically spent on stages doing acting in theatre plays or sitting in the audience, admiring his screenplay for the same. When his pen isn't breathing life into blank papers, he can be either found backpacking in the Himalayas with his loyal comrade camera or dribbling the ball on the basketball court.

He has written short stories for anthologies as well as articles for various magazines. He has also authored a

fiction book titled ‘Maybe Yes’ which was featured on - Top 100 books to read on Amazon India.

He can be reached via:
Email: author.abhijeet@gmail.com
Instagram: instagram.com/abhii_kumar
Facebook: facebook.com/abhijeet.fd

INFINITE LOVE

The onset of dusk was pulling me to gaze at the horizon where the green fields could be seen merging with the blue skies, but just then a fading voice startled me.
"Something was cooking between you and her, isn't it?" A bewildering moment struck me after hearing the sentence under the influence of marijuana.
"What are you talking about?" I asked.
"Between you and Rhea," Yash said, puffing a joint.
"Why do you say that?" I asked, ignoring the last infant rays of the yellow ball finding the shelter behind the Himalayan foothills of Mussoorie.
"I don't know; we always used to have a gossip about you guys," Yash said, passing me the joint.
"Say what?" I asked, puffing the joint.
"You were always protective of her, everybody noticed. You looked at her differently. "He said with a grim smile which I noticed from the corner of my eye.
I was dumbstruck for a moment and did not utter a single word. Am I in love with her? Is it too late to confess? I asked myself. There was no answer from my conscience, or maybe I chose not to confront it. The relationship which I share with her has no name; or I chose to make it that way without her, although I knew the fact that I still feel for her, adore her and care for her. I fucking love her!
"What is stopping you from telling her? It has been more than 2 years" Yash said and walked off.
"Just Say it!" My mind said. My inner subconscious fell into limbo, and I just stood there looking at her. One thing was sure I cannot let her go, even if I wanted to. I wanted to be with her; to feel her. I want to fill the spaces between my fingers with hers.

“What is about me that makes me so unreal at times? Why can’t I let go? I whispered, looking towards the sky filled with shimmering stars.

“You feel infinite with her.” The stars answered back.

“They are going to close the gates, let’s go,” Yash yelled from a distance. I knelt on my knees and placed her favourite white lilies on her grave.

“I love you, Rhea, I always had. See you on the other side.” I whispered and followed Yash towards the cemetery gate.

ACHAL MOGLA

Achal Mogla is an author and an avid reader by heart. He belongs from Agra - Taj Mahal City of India and has explored places like Ahmedabad and Gujarat for quite a long time in his life. He has released three of his books with the latest one 'Where did I Goof Up in Life? Living life without excuses' being released recently. You won't like to miss the splendid messages that he has delivered. His first book 'Salt and Pepper' has touched hearts with its romantic short stories. His second book 'The Revival' was a book written for young minds. Being a hobbyist reader and writer, Achal has written over 200+ poems and prose for his reader audience and you can read them through his social media channels. He has participated in over 15 different anthologies and continues doing so. Achal is a B.Tech in Dairy Technology from

SMC College of Dairy Science and a post-graduate in Management with specialisation in Human Resources from Symbiosis School, Pune. He loves interacting with people and meeting new people. He is crazy about reading books and he has a huge collection of books. Apart from reading books which is his passion and hobby, he loves to write poems, loves hanging out with friends, loves eating out food at new places and is also a certified Handwriting Analyst!

UNFINISHED DREAMS

Sonu lived with his Mom and Dad. There was a difference not visible to the naked eye though his parents, like every other parent, always did their best to fulfil the demands of their only son. Sonu was a mature child despite being so young. His father was a farmer and mother, a housewife. Books fascinated Sonu since childhood. Irony was that he could not attend school. His parents could not afford the fees yet they managed to get him books to study. He used to help his father at the farm and he had seen him toil effortlessly from morning till late evening in the blazing sun. After a hard day's work Sonu would finish his dinner and study under the street lamp. Since books were his passion no one could stop him from gaining knowledge. He would undertake paid work for three to four hours and give the money to his parents to meet household expenses. His parents knew Sonu's passion for knowledge and they wanted him to become a professor in a famous college and this was the common unfinished dream of all three. Three factors which differentiated Sonu from others -his passion, his willpower and his end goal. Sonu always knew that a day would come when his unfinished dream would see the light of the day. He kept studying. While working he was able to save his salary and it helped him get into a good school and eventually into college. Sonu had already made up his mind that he would take up teaching as his profession and seek employment in one of the best colleges. Eventually he become a teacher in IIM Ahmedabad which was amongst the best and the fact that he was doing what he loved gave him a feeling of *deja vu*. Later that month as Sonu got his first salary cheque he went home to present it to his parents as their dream had been fulfilled too. Sonu had started from scratch and rose to become the faculty in

one of the most prestigious colleges in the city. It was indeed a story from rags to riches but it would not have been possible without the hard work, perseverance, willpower and dedication. This helped Sonu convert the 'Unfinished dream' into a finished one.

KAVITHA ARJUN

Not only a Software professional and a Lawyer, Kavitha Arjun is also an avid Writer, chasing her dream and passion for writing! Her debut fiction, 'The Mystery Repeats' gained positive reviews and was ranked #1 bestseller in Kindle under Mysteries. Her second book 'Tales with a Twist' is gaining good recognition. Now she presents to you, her comic short story "The wedding invitation".

THE WEDDING INVITATION

Unknown number: "Hello" "Hello. Is it Nisha?" "Yes! Who is this?" Hey, Nisha. This is Lokesh here. Remember me?" (Surprised) Hey, Lokesh. How can I forget you? How have you been? Long-time man! So what's happening? Lokesh was my UG classmate. My best friend Shruti and Lokesh were in relationship but Lokesh ditched her. I was wondering, why on earth would Lokesh call me? "Nisha, I'm getting married. Hmmm it all happened in a blink… Family's pressure! Moreover, these days it's very hard to find a good match. Hmmm, can you give me your address?"Lokesh asked me so casually. How can this guy be so cool after ruining my friend's life? "Hey, Congratulations! It's ok, just send me a WhatsApp message" I was hesitant. "Hey come on. No formalities. I want to invite you in person!" Lokesh insisted. "Ok! I'll text you" I ended the call. I initiated a group call with my girlfriends. "Lokesh? Why did he call you?" "I have no idea. Should I tell Shruti?" I checked. "Not a good idea. She is still not out of the shock" my friend warned me. "What was the real issue?" she asked. "Some sort of misunderstanding. But he told her that he's not ready for marriage. He was not on social media" I told them. Talking for about an hour of their love story, we couldn't digest the fact that he had ditched our best friend. We wanted to somehow insult him. We made a 'Master Plan' Lokesh was about to arrive! I was standing near the gate, looking inside and outside and talking to myself. Everyone was ready with rotten tomatoes and eggs. He approached my house. I signalled my friends. As he came inside the gate to park his bike, scraps started flying from all sides. I waved, howled and cried to stop! But the flow was never ending. He then walked towards me fully soiled, looking at me awfully. My friends came closer to abuse him but they stopped abruptly. “Meet Logesh, my school senior!” I giggled. I totally forgot this guy, Logesh alias Logeshwaran, with whom I walked back from school every day. We convinced Logesh that it was meant to be a prank and apologized for our behaviour .Always keep your picture as display on WhatsApp to avoid confusions. Let’s all wish Logesh a Happy Married Life.

NITIN SHARMA

Nitin Sharma is a successful author of two books namely 'The other side of love and wardrobe malfunction' (kindle e-book). With a collection of around 700 paperbacks and 2000 e-books he's a passionate reader and blogger. He lives in Uttar Pradesh with his family and is presently teaching in a government college.

You can send him your love and feedback to:

Authornittin@gmail.com

Instagram handle @Authornittin

SHE'S MINE..... FOREVER

"Hi! Aman" Aman was watching the sun disappearing below the horizon when he heard his name being called. He turned abruptly to find a familiar face staring at him. "Reva! My God", he said unable to mask his shock. "Punch me if I'm not dreaming." "You're not! I'm very much real", she said calmly. "You here? Last time I checked, you were in Gurgaon, happily married." "I was but my husband died in a car accident three months ago. A drunken truck driver ran over his car. He died on the spot." "I'm sorry. I didn't know," Aman said apologetically. "Anything I could do," he trailed off… "It's okay and Yes. I'm here to ask a favour. I've heard that you're opening a restaurant and need a partner to assist." "Yes." "You think I'm qualified enough to be your partner?" "Reva," Aman said taking her hands in his. "We broke up on a happy note. Your parents were against our union and I respected that. We weren't meant to be life partners but I'm sure we'd be great business partners." "Thank you!" Reva said managing a sad smile. It took them three months to start the restaurant and another six to turn it into one of Delhi's finest. They finally settled into a comfort zone, suppressing their past emotions but emotions could find a million routes to escape and once they did, they're unstoppable. They were still in love or at least Aman was. It was on Valentine's Day. The restaurant was filled to capacity. Aman strapped his guts, stood on top of a table and proposed Reva. Reva took no time to say yes, like she had been waiting for it all this while. Their marriage was short and simple affair but they complemented it with a week-long honeymoon in Paris. The way Aman's love was heading, he was on cloud nine and then the call came. "Hello! Aman sir," the voice said. "I'm out on bail. Your lawyer proved that the other guy

was drunk while driving." "Good. Your two million will reach you by nightfall as promised. Enough to keep your mouth shut." "Of course! What should I do with the truck?" "Sell it, burn it or push it down the mountain top. It doesn't matter anymore. I have achieved what I desired." 'SHE'S MINE FOREVER.'

JEENA R. PAPAADI

Jeena R. Papaadi writes short stories, novels and poems. Her published works include Shadows of the Past (stories), Temple of Time (novel), Tales from the Garden City (stories) and Lonely Journeys (poems). Jeena's story 'Houses of God' was among the six stories by Indian authors featured in 'Wisdom of Our Mothers: Indian Edition,' published by Familia Books, USA, in 2011. Her story 'Land of the Pure' was shortlisted in Juggernaut publishers' short story contest in 2018. Three of her short stories were in the top ten of The MAG India's short story contest in 2010 and are featured in 'Nude and Other Stories' published by The MAG (theMAG.in). Jeena lives in Bangalore, India, with her husband and son.

She can be reached via-
Instagram @jeenapapaadi
Twitter @jeenapapaadi

THE WOMAN IN WHITE

The old woman, draped in a crumpled white cotton saree, sat absolutely still. The pallu carelessly pulled around her and dug into her waist showed no sign of ever having encountered irons. Her glasses rested on the edge of her nose. A woman older than she was sprawled on the sofa, fanning herself. A young man sat watching cricket on television. His sister was turning the pages of a magazine without seeing anything, her legs raised on her seat. Dusk had fallen. There was nothing to do but wait for dinner. The old woman in white hugged her arms, eyebrows raised in concentration, her eyes surreptitiously drifting here and there, all around her. She would look up when spoken to and sometimes grunt a reply, clearl The old woman, draped in a crumpled white cotton saree, sat absolutely still. The *pallu* carelessly pulled around her and dug into her waist showed no sign of ever having encountered ironing. Her glasses rested on the edge of her nose. Another woman, older than her, sprawled on the sofa fanning herself. A young man sat watching cricket on television. His sister was turning the pages of a magazine without seeing anything, her legs raised on her seat. Dusk had fallen. There was nothing to do but wait for dinner. The old woman in white hugged her arms, eyebrows raised in concentration, her eyes surreptitiously drifting here and there, all around her. She would look up when spoken to and sometimes grunt a reply, clearly not approving of the disturbance. She would wave her hands at times, like a traffic policeman directing vehicles. At other times, she sat as though she were frozen. About half an hour passed thus. The youngster shifted in his seat as the match progressed, deep intakes of breath giving away the fate of his team. The flip-flap of the newspaper fanning the older woman, the lazy rustle of the magazine in the young

woman's hands and the groans of the ancient fan provided the background to the television commentary. A light drizzle and a distant rumble suggested the possibility of a storm later in the night. Then… A subtle change came over the woman in white. She remained immobile but her eyes narrowed and began darting with rapt attention. Her fingers rubbed against each other, to warm up for the final act. Slowly, very slowly, she drew her feet closer to her. *Slap*! The older woman stopped fanning and stared. The youngster muted the TV and whirled around. The young woman gaped, the magazine dropping from her hands. Her eyes betraying a suggestion of glee, the White Woman opened her closed palms and slowly pulled out something small and black between her thumb and index finger. With a triumphant face, she held it out to the others for a second before flicking it away. "Darn mosquito!" she said.

JIHAN K PATEL

Jihan Patel, a 17 year old writer based in Ahmedabad, Gujarat has written 2 books based on superheroes. His 1st book 'Mystery of Mystical man' has written at the age of 12 and he has gone on to write his 2nd book 'Mystical man: Revenge of Orion' which was published by 'The Write Place' in April 2019 which consists of 59000 words.

THE ARTIST

Jenny Malhotra was a young Indian girl probably in her mid-twenties. She was a tenant in a small apartment near the airport. Due to the current covid-19 situation she had lost her job in the IT industry as her company faced a huge financial crisis compelling them to fire some of their employees. The fact that her boyfriend Ricky Singh broke up with her, further added fuel to the fire. It was her first break-up until now. Depressed and desperate, Jenny was lying on the sofa and crying. Her crying stopped, and she went into a *boketto*. She thought about why she was crying over the loss of her job when she didn't even like it that much. Her dream was to become an artist but her family had forced her to become an IT engineer. And the break-up was not her fault at all. She thought, 'I always wanted to become an artist and paint for a living. And now as I am free from the bondage of my job and relationship so why not start my own you-tube channel…' Without further ado, she opened her not-so-used cupboard, took out some oil paint tubes, a palette, few canvases, some brushes, a canvas stand, and paint thinner. She set up the canvas on the stand, and used a phone stand to shoot herself in the process of drawing. She chose the reference image, drew a rough outline, took some colours on the palette and started painting. Jenny loved art because drawing would teleport her into a different dimension, it was ecstasy for her and she was never tired of it. She doesn't need to plan a drawing; it mostly came automatically to her. Dexterously she took the colours and started applying them on the canvas. A novice would think that she was randomly applying colour. Every stroke, every moment of her hand was subconscious, nothing was forced and everything was automatic and then she would stop to take a look, start

again and get lost in the process. After many hours her painting was finally completed, a masterpiece. Jenny felt a sense of satisfaction, a sense of ecstasy as if all her sorrows were gone and she was free to do what she wanted to. Art was her healer, her ecstasy, and now became her way to make a living.

NAMIT

Namit is working as a Software Manager in Vadodara, Gujarat. He has published his first book named, 'The Broken Guitar- A tale of two friends' in 2020 during pandemic. Apart from writing computer programs and fictional stories, he follows other passions like pencil sketching, travelling, gardening, reading history/biographies/religious books and takes a keen interest in sports like cricket and tennis.

THE BEGINNING

Strained married life, almost at the verge of a divorce and work pressure was taking a toll on my mind, heart, and soul. For the world, Mohan was one of the most successful entrepreneurs. But inside me, only I knew how empty I was! Meera, my personal assistant, a single mother was my punching bag, occasionally bruising her soul with my taunting words. But, never did she complain about my rude behaviour nor the laborious tasks that I kept piling on her while she kept her personal issues at bay. Sensing that I was lost deep in my troubling thoughts, she came towards me with a glass of water and my routine medicines. Although it satisfied my thirst I was thankless. My ego was bigger than my self-introspection. My personal life failures turned a joyous me to an emotionless snobbish boss. I asked her to read some sealed letters on my desk. Unfortunately, the first letter she opened was a divorce letter from my wife which made us to stare at each other with disbelief and pain. That moment I was ruined completely and left for home without uttering a single word. Two hearts were broken that day. I could see that in her eyes. I was in a self-exile, I was shattered completely. None of my close friends, colleagues or family members bothered about my existence. But surprisingly, there was Meera. She was the only person who would text me twice a day, just to remind me about my medicines. Maybe she just wanted to know whether I was alright. I could feel that. How many people are there in your life that take care of you selflessly in your worst time even though you have been so rude to them all your life? Meera was that person for me. It was one stormy and rainy night when I went back to work after a couple of weeks of an emotional breakdown. With the fear of getting late for home, she was constantly

keeping an eye on the weather. I wanted to do something for her. While she was just above to leave, I called her, "Meera...". She turned her head around, and looked at me. "If you don't mind, can I drop you home..."? She lowered her eyes and smiled. That long drive with Meera amidst rainfall was the ‘beginning’ of my happiness.

VINEET AHLAWAT

The author Vineet Ahlawat is a veterinary sciences graduate from Haryana and has developed passion for writing during his college days. His ability to carve out a special niche is adequately highlighted in his novel works like ‘An Anonymous Guy’ and several screenplays titled ‘Aiyyaz, My Dream’, ‘Patriotism’ and ‘Safed Kagaz.

ROOTS OF PEACE

"What are you doing, Amu?" asked Mahmud, plastering the manger meant for the flock of sheep. "Abbu you are so silly, this is the sapling of peace. It will represent growth and peace in our country." Amu grinned and walked away. "I am sorry my child. But yes! This one is really beautiful like you." Mahmud embraced the little leaves of the sapling. Amu, now a grown up woman walks at her full pace towards her house. As she hustles amid the barren land, she notices a convoy of tanks moving towards west. She is panting heavily, yet moving unstoppably. She reaches her town and enters inside her house forcibly throwing away curtain at the entrance to a side. Her siblings are watching news on the television and glance towards her as she enters. "What did they say?" asked Amu, making a seat for herself among the crowd. We have talked with the Taliban and the other stakeholders to promote peace in the upcoming days of this decade. Our troops will be moving out of Afghanistan by September 11, 2021." Secretary of State for the United States spoke at the Afghan Peace Deal. "We believe that in Afghanistan there shall be a government that honours the Islamic laws and regulations. And yes, Afghan will flourish for sure but the definition of 'flourishing state' will be according to us." A representative of Taliban responded to the statement. After a couple of months, Amu is watering her 'peace sapling' which now has grown into a 20-year old tree. Meanwhile one day, a rally of Taliban troops enters the town raging ahead and speeding on their jeeps. As they come near, one of them drives his jeep rashly, crashing the edge of the jeep into the peace tree. Amu hastily steps backwards, stumbles and fall down. She realises that the tree has fallen down to the ground and the jeep has fled leaving behind a storm of dust. Amu sighs

heavily with tears in her eyes and says, “The roots of peace are short lived.” She lies down near the tree and closes her eyes.

SRIPREMRAJ

Sripremraj Sinnaiah, Author of 'Retrospective Wellness Series - Book I' lives in Kuala Lumpur, Malaysia. He is a wellness enthusiast with over 10 years of experience in this industry. He has created his wellness start-up and hope to make wellness (services & products) an affordable lifestyle for everyone. He actively pursues Martial arts, Varmakalai, Sidda medicine and sports.

DON'T REACT, RESPOND!!!

It was a busy weekday morning and the whole city was bustling with cars. Rahul was driving his car with his mind pre occupied by the intense argument he had had with his wife earlier that morning. As Rahul left the house, he knew what his wife said was true but was too righteous to accept it. Suddenly there was a bang followed by a blast of horns and the accident brought Rahul's thoughts back to the road. By the time he realized what had happened it was too late. He had banged into a car in front. The victim's car was an E-class Mercedes and an elegantly dressed gentleman got down. He wore professional attire symbolizing his status. He walked towards Rahul with a firm gait and as he reached out, Rahul stepped out with a grim face and started cursing the situation trying to put the blame on everything. He even cursed the gentleman accusing him of not being careful. "I am terribly sorry. It was my mistake to have not noticed your car. I understand you are in a very bad mood already, so please take my card and reach out when you have tackled your impending urgent matters. I will be happy to connect later on" saying this, the gentleman passed on his card and reached out for a handshake with a warm smile. Rahul was taken aback by the way the gentleman responded, took the card and slowly reached out for a handshake. Then he read the card and realization hit him hard. The gentleman standing in front was one of the most influential business men in the city. When he looked up, the gentleman was already walking towards his car. Rahul ran towards the gentleman and pleaded for forgiveness. The gentleman still walking replied "There is this one important lesson I have learnt through hardships, 'Don't React, Respond'. If you can understand this you won't have to be sorry next time." With that the gentleman got into his car and left leaving Rahul dumbstruck. After a few days of thought Rahul realized the importance of those words. If the gentleman had reacted by taking on the fight, he would have wasted the most important asset of all… 'TIME' and also, that move would have had negative repercussions throughout his day. Instead, he simply responded with a positive note controlling the outcome and hence winning the situation.

SHAIWAL

Shaiwal is a name with Persian roots defining uniqueness and honesty, and so is she, a hardworking soul with decisive brain who believes in spreading happiness all around. More importantly, she is a chatterbox who has many friends. Believing in the process, she has achieved her dream of pursuing Masters in Literature after becoming an Electronics Engineer. She strives to raise voice against child sex abuse.

HOMEWORK

"Bhaiya, do not go to the coaching class today", she said to her brother while going to sleep, after a tiring day at school. Raniya and her elder brother, Naksh stayed back at home with their uncle, while their parents were away at work. On that fateful day, she had returned from school, changed her clothes and ate her lunch just like any other normal day. Then she had gone to sleep with her brother lying beside her. She was a very sincere child who listened to her elders. But that day, she was not feeling safe, rather her instinct was telling her something bad was about to happen. In the evening, she woke up all of a sudden, sweating and trembling in fear. Her underpants were wet, the uncle sat beside her, looking at his prey with tempting eyes. Moving close, he inappropriately touched her. She was scared as hell and totally helpless. But suddenly the phone rang in the other room and the uncle unwillingly went to attend it. Meanwhile, Raniya got a chance to hide below the bed. The nightmare returned with the uncle, who started looking all around the room and was soon able to find her hideout. She resisted being dragged out, but to no avail. The uncle pulled her underpants down and started with the long-awaited business of lust and pleasure. After that, he threw her in the corner and asked her to keep quiet; else he assured that he would give her a good thrashing the next day. After a few hours, all the family members returned. Raniya was crying in the room when her mother came looking for her. She immediately got up to hug her, but the uncle came in and said, "I scolded her for not completing Maths homework and since then she is crying". Raniya stared blankly at her mother who said, "There is no excuse for not studying, from tomorrow onwards Rajesh uncle will teach you Maths every day". Two months later, Raniya failed in Maths.

SANDEEP BOGRA

Sandeep Bogra is a best-selling author on Amazon for his unique book: Divorce - The Best Thing Ever Happened? He is also a motivational speaker, life & relationship coach. Being 'passionate about people' and striving to add value to your life and relationships, Sandeep founded 'Someone Listening' in 2012. He is a catalyst for change! His tailor-made seminars and key-note presentations influence thinking-patterns and impact lives positively and undivided attention to your innermost feelings during one-on-one coaching empowers you to make informed decisions and achieve results. He is a certified life coach from Tony

Robbins – Madanes Training centre, Neuro Linguistic Programming (NLP) practitioner and an approved counsellor. He is also certified in business communication skills from Dale Carnegie Training. Sandeep is also a Chartered Accountant from ICAI & an executive MBA (Finance) from Institute of Management Technology, Ghaziabad. He started his career at McKinsey & Company and gained a decade of management consulting experience in India and Middle East. He is a dog-lover, philanthropist and a member of Rotary International Club. His burning desire: 'Touch & Transform Lives for the Better...'

THE 'UNFAIR' FAREWELL…

With the college farewell planned for the next day, Sam went from pillar to post; unable to find a unique gift for the love of his eye. As he mustered the strength to finally speak his heart, Sam's dream girl seemed missing on the last day. None but Sam could ever realize that there is no tomorrow, a thought which kept him from stepping up every day. She had never bunked till date, rather urged him to be regular, as Sam and Kelly shared a great bond of friendship. Always so close, yet so far; she never saw it in his eyes, and was invisible herself today. His heart skipped a beat, when clueless and dismayed Sam kept calling her switched-off phone. Such a shy guy couldn't enquire from her friends either. "Should I visit her place?" He thought. Zooming at full throttle, he landed at her locked door; ringing the doorbell repeatedly, pleading for a miracle from the Heavens above. However, she was still nowhere in sight. With eyes full of tears and mind lost in loneliness, Sam's car got overturned by a truck on his way back home. He lost all his senses yet murmured Kelly's name all the way in the ambulance. An apple a day keeps the doctor away. If the nurse is cute, forget the fruit. Months passed by in his inert state of coma, with no signs of recovery, until there was a new discovery. A young nurse joined the hospital and Sam's body started to respond to this familiar face. Yes, something ticked inside him and he was finally revived, until this fairy left the hospital with no signs of return to call of her duty, rather magic to cure Sam's disability. His wavering hands shivered, eyes rolled upside down, his heart pulsated so rapidly that he fell off the bed with a thud and the glass jar of water lying on his bedside smashed into pieces. The impact was indeed very powerful,

when Kelly splashed water on Sam's eyes, only to wake him up again and bid farewell to his unfair nightmare…

RASHMI CHAND

Rashmi Chand is a content writer, micro-influencer and a Hotel and Hospitality training professional. She shares her motherhood experiences at 'www.notjustmommying.com' and has also authored a fun book for children called 'The Teethbugs and The Bunny'.

SLEEPING BEAUTY

Newlywed Anamika looked lovely in the bright outfit adorning her slender frame. A big red *bindi*, glittering vermillion-red *sindoor* on her forehead and the bright red *chooda* till her elbows, all this put together, made her look nothing short of a Goddess in a *Durga Pandal*. All her new family members were smitten by her beauty but there was something amiss, something inexplicable about her big beautiful eyes that looked dreamy all the time. Rohan often sang romantic Hindi songs in praises of her intoxicating beautiful big eyes that mirrored the depth of an ocean but all she did was smile and turn him away. It had been few weeks into the marriage and Anamika was still a girl of few words. Everyone thought her to be an introvert, taking yet some more time to gel with people in her new world. They gave her her space and time and she preferred to stay in her room or sit in the cosy patio in their lush green lawn, sipping her green tea and looking into nowhere, lost in her thoughts. She was different in more ways than what people would have liked. She often slept longer than expected, at unexpected hours, so much so that her new family thought she was being plain lazy. However, her husband didn't mind anything about his sleeping beauty; he happily snuggled up next to her and watched her with a content smile as she lay smiling in her slumber. With each passing day she slept longer and longer until one day she slept so much so as to not wake up ever. She was found perfectly still with a bottle of potent pills next to her. Her dreams took her away from her reality, her dreams took her to a place she met her lover, relived the past and fulfilled all her desires.

BILAL K SHAIKH

Bilal K. Shaikh is a start-up co-founder, team leader and an educational social worker working in SaaS product development. He is a chapter secretary of a national NGO. Apart from that, he had a keen interest in literature, theology and philosophy from an early age and had studied the subjects very actively. His research paper on *"Branding and its effects"* is been selected for top journals and his innovative ideas to solve real world problems have been recognized by many different organizations.

A BRIEF REFLECTION IN THE PASSING MOMENT

It felt like yesterday, his old voice struck my ears and prompted me to wake up and do something about my life. It almost carried me out on a journey of growth like I was looking for the hope inside me that enables the possibility of doing something worthwhile. I was silent without an answer to his call, I think he might have heard inside that I am awake, like a few moments ago, I did. That young fellow, so talented in his work but not being able to achieve his potential and when I threw some powerful lines at him, he felt it. It was again silent and I knew he woke up.

Like that first time, when I deeply admired that girl, I adored her and romanticized the entire interaction, but when she broke my heart it was unbearable and I even thought "how can someone be so cold-hearted?", but then I'm ashamed of being that cold-hearted person too, who broke a few hearts himself, who didn't care about the feelings of others.

In an audience of hundreds, when that speaker spoke truth of his life so confidently and inspired many, I was one among them who looked up to him as an idol and thought he was worth following as a mentor. However, recently when I stood on stage with a crowd who looked at me with so much hope of imbibing my preaching, I had this guilt that I entitled myself to the stage with unreal underlying lies.

An employee of my company came to me with tears in his eyes and told me about the success in his recent project just because I guided him through it by sparing my 'Now Valuable' time. Similar to that, my first boss had helped me build my confidence with his experience and shed light on how to find the true self within me.

It is all a big circle, like a joker in the circus keeps juggling objects that keep coming back to him again and again, similarly it reminds me that life is really a process which sometimes happens to you and sometimes you make it happen to others. And I hope that I have played my role properly like those who had played a part in the chapters of my life's book.

ANANYAA SALVE

Ananyaa is a creative young girl, who likes to pursue art in various forms. She loves to paint, write and dance and has a special place in her heart for baking cakes. She spends most of her time setting up her goals and working towards them. Ananyaa aspires to be a renowned artist and looks forward to inspire young girls to follow their dreams.

"UNBOUNDED CAMARADERIE"

Leisha hurries to her room and changes her clothes. She puts on some pyjamas, a sweater and pink socks and lies down in her bed. She hates leaving the house, even if for business.
She only goes to school by bus and returns home to be by herself. She prefers to sit at home and spend her time devouring books, painting portraits or listening to jazz.
She tucks herself in the blankets and picks up her book from her bedside table. She opens it to right where she left it last. She can't concentrate, for her mind is elsewhere. All she can think about is the boy's eyes from the bus.
They were wonderful. She was completely enraptured by how surreal the moment was. She had shifted her gaze from his eyes to his slightly up-turned nose and then to his pink lips.
"How can one be so perfect?" She thought to herself.
He seemed very silent. He got on the bus, bought a ticket and chose the window seat right beside Leisha. Something was definitely intimidating about this boy. She glanced at him a couple of times, trying to take in how beautiful he was. The boy seemed to be very quiet throughout the ride.
The next day, she waited eagerly for the school to finish. She took the bus and after three stops, there he was. He climbed aboard, bought a ticket and sat beside her. Leisha curiously asked him "Hi. What's your name?"
At first, he was startled. But he smiled and said "I'm Agasthya. How are you doing Leisha?"
"How do you know my name?"
"Umm, you have a nametag on your bag." They both chuckled. After talking about a billion random things, they both went home happy to have made a new friend that day.
Day after day, Leisha and Agasthya gained each other's trust and love. It turned out that Agasthya had a similar nature to

that of Leisha and he loved to read books and paint. The way both of them perceived the world in their own way was mesmerising. They started going on little trips to Ice cream shops or to Momo outlets.

Gradually, both of them realized that they were truly themselves when they were with each other. This wasn't friendship nor was this love. It was a sweet little bond. Only they knew how precious it was.

SAURAV RANJAN DATTA

Saurav Ranjan Datta is an author who has written for Hindustan Times, CNBCTV18, Timeless Travels Magazine UK, Outlook India, Times Journal, Ancient Origins Magazine, Ancient History Encyclopedia, Sulekha.com, Utkal Today, The Assam Tribune and The Indian Hour. He is also the author of books like 'Maidens of Fate' and 'Where Bravehearts Dwelt.' He has also been part of anthologies like 'Harmonious Symphonies' & 'Fragrances of Life.'

THE SUDDEN STRANGER

How Tanush had hoped that this year would be a quiet one for him after all the mayhem of the last year, which saw a minister being assassinated by her bodyguards. Their house had become a melting pot for all political discussions then, with his uncles visiting Papa almost every day. Tanush did not like all that noise and chatter, as he would delve deep into the world of storybooks after school. He loved the silence of his home, which was situated off the main road, on an undulating valley. Even the streets remained deserted in their quaint hometown. Tanush had a simple routine. After school, he would often visit the library, borrow his favourite author's books and after reaching home, would do nothing until he had finished that novel. His favourite author's name was Christopher Bond, who wrote primarily bone-chilling detective stories for children, but the author never shared his photograph in those books. Life was going fine for them until one fine day when their hometown was rocked by a rumour about the appearance of a Criminal who kidnapped and murdered children.

"Remember Tanush, come back home early." His mother warned him one morning, as he was getting ready for school. That afternoon, the streets seemed eerily silent. As Tanush took the first bend towards his home, he saw a bearded man standing beneath the bus stand wearing dark goggles. The man looked at Tanush and gave a smile. As soon as he crossed, Tanush heard him saying, *"Listen kid, I have something to ask."* Tanush started perspiring and after remembering something, quickened his pace. However, the man too started walking towards him. After some time, Tanush almost started running and could hear the man shouting, *"Hey kid, listen please."* As soon as he reached home, Tanush heaved a sigh of relief. But he did not

mention anything to his mom and went to sleep, exhausted. When he got up, he saw his parents watching TV. Just then, the TV hostess announced the name of the person whom she was going to interview. Tanush jumped with joy to hear the name of Christopher Bond. As soon as the man came into view, the young boy stood shell-shocked to see his favourite author's face. It was the bearded man from the afternoon. Little did Tanush know that the author was on a visit to his town!

SHILPA SALVE

Shilpa Salve is a Yoga instructor, professionally trained by Yoga & Ayurveda Prabodhini & Vishwa Yoga School and Research Centre. She is also a certified Life Coach by Arfeen Khan. She has been learning yoga since the age of 13, and has worked with various institutes and coaching centres all along the way. As a Mind and Body Wellness Coach and the Founder of 'Empowering Yog', she has impacted over 1000 lives in the last decade. Shilpa aspires to assist people, break through their physical and mental

difficulties that hinder them from living a life of true meaning and wonderful experiences. Her mission is to influence people and create more awareness towards self-empowerment, self-confidence and self-realization. She has co-authored a book 'Cut the Crap'. Writing is her passion and she has also written a poetry collection in Hindi by the name 'Chahatein Kuch Unkahisi' .She can be reached via
https://www.facebook.com/shilpa.salve
Insta handle @shilpz.dreamz
Website: www.empoweringyog.com

MOTHER KNOWS THE BEST

I throw myself on the chair outside the ICU frightened and exhausted. I think about the last hour which brought me here, having seen these images only on the television before. Hospital's emergency services, ambulance carrying critical patients, doctors and medics running to treat them and relatives of the patients standing helplessly and hoping for miracles. All this is happening right in front of my eyes and I am totally transported to a different world. Sitting on that chair holding my head in my hands, I think of how I felt when I thought I might lose my mother today. But by God's grace I was able to get timely help. Here she was, lying in ICU with all the equipment attached; pricking her veins, monitor beeping and constantly changing numbers on the screen. I am not able to handle that stress and holding myself together just to convince myself how strong I am even though this is hardly true. This is after doctors assure me they have started the treatment and I'm hoping she'll get well soon. You don't realize what you've got until you lose it. That is human nature. That day I realized what it will be to lose my mother, '*Aai*'. *Aai* and I unlike any other mother-daughter never shared any special bond and I had never connected with her when it came to sharing my emotions, thoughts or desires. She has been a different mother and been very strict and particular about my good behaviour. This has always felt like a burden, provoking my rebellious nature. We always had clashes about almost everything. But today I am stunned at the thought of losing her and have realized her importance in my life. When thinking from this perspective I discovered that though she was never a soft and loving mother like my friends' mothers, her aggression to make me perfect has made me a better person. It is because of her uncommon upbringing that I am an independent, courageous and a strong woman now. Today when she is in the hospital, I am being a mother to her. I have to be stern with her about doing things which may pose to be harmful for her health. I have to coerce her to follow certain instructions and rules for the betterment of her health. Oh! How the tables have turned.

RIMA SEN

Rima is a creative artist who is a hopeless romantic. Growing up in a secluded village by the sea, she completed her Master's from Coventry University, UK. A former cabin crew and a globetrotter, she is inspired by the magic of nature and the innate goodness in people. She believes that every person is a story worth writing about. She embraces every aspect of her life with a touch of gratitude and a positive outlook. Having lived close to Nature for most parts of her life, she weaves her stories with a refreshing blend of nature, suspense, humour and romance.

THE CHASE

As I was shopping for the Children's Bible at the Pauline gift shop, I was suddenly aware of a pair of eyes following me. Call it a woman's intuition. After I paid and rushed out, I was still aware of being followed. This is not common in a city like Mumbai in broad daylight. I hurried. Hearing a panting voice calling out, I was taken aback with what I saw. For the first time ever, I was being followed by a woman and not a man. I halted. This lady did not resemble anyone I knew. She was a fair-complexioned, middle-aged lady and I couldn't help myself from admiring the bright green silk saree she was wearing. She stood across me and smiled. "*Malayalee aan*?" I politely replied that I did not know Malayalam. Her heart sank but she quickly masked her disappointment and proceeded to the next question. "Oh, no problem. You Christian? I saw you pick Bible in store." "Yes aunty, I am a Christian." Her *kohled* eyes immediately sparkled. She beamed. "My son is thirty years, ma. Very handsome. Working in BKC, an MNC and earning very well", she lilted with a heavy Malayali accent and broken English. By now I understood why I was being followed, as I controlled my laughter. I kept calm. I was dealing with a mom here. I could clearly see a mother's desperation for her son from the eyes which looked at me expectantly. "My daughter is in the third grade aunty", I sheepishly told her. She was visibly embarrassed and I didn't like the look of guilt which appeared on her face. After all, I am a mother myself. "Wherever God has planned, he will get married aunty", I consoled her. She smiled a pure genuine mother's smile. "You have lovely hair, ma." "Thank you, aunty", I said as I touched my heart and waved goodbye. I will forever remember her face. A mother who almost proposed marriage for her son on her first meeting with a girl who wore a knee length dress. Only a mom's love can be so innocent. Even as I lay down to sleep, her face flashed across making me giggle. That son must be very lucky to have a mother like this. And whomsoever he gets married to, I am sure of one thing; his mom will prove to be an amazing mother-in-law.

VIJAYALATHA N

Vijayalatha is an inquisitive seeker and forever explorer who loves being in the nature. Extra sensory perception, astral travel, cognition, telekinesis, time and cosmic consciousness are the subjects that are of interest to her. The practice of penning down experiences from her travels, treks, sports adventure and day to day activities inspired her to venture into writing. Her other books are 'The Involution' and 'The Divine frequency 2020.'

THE BYGONE

Sitting by a small river stream Mayura was watching the mesmerizing twilight of the dusk when a glimpse of a dark figure standing on the other side of the stream caught her attention. It stood stock-still amidst the tranquillity of the gloomy sky, subtle winds carrying the scent of leaves and the sound of steadily moving river.

"Hello? Can you hear me?" uttered Mayura

The dark figure trudged down the stream, "What's your Name kid?"

"Mayura"

"You should not be here, It's not safe!"

"You seem to be a good human? Why are you here? Searching for someone?"

"What are you doing here?" enquired the man in harsh tone

"Waiting"

"For whom"

"Father"

"Is he lost here?"

"Everyone is lost somewhere, the question is will they find themselves"

"Wise for your age! You must be like 18 or 19? My daughter is your age……"

"What happened to your daughter?"

"Hmmm! In my profession I have more enemies than friends. About two months ago, she was kidnapped by the hooligans. Chopped smithereens of a body with her college ID card was sent to my home. My heart didn't accept that it was my daughter, so I never stopped looking for her. A week ago tribals in here spotted a girl with her features"

"Did you find the hooligans who caused this?"

“Their bodies were found in this forest, strange as it could be they were not hurt or diseased. Tribals believe that it’s their peacock deity who punished them”
“What do you think?
It’s a sham! Why didn’t it save my wife or my daughter and many innocent people?”
“In your role as a cop do you kill everyone?”
“No! Can’t do it without evidence! Some are innocent and some do change with guidance”
“So might be this deity!”
“You speak highly of this one! Typical tribe”
“Well, It’s time for me to go” said Mayura
“Your father is here?”
“I never said it’s my father! You should head straight to the ancient tree. An old tribe will guide you”, she said pointing fingers in the trees direction
“Wait! How did you know am a cop? As the man turned back, Mayura was bygone .He strode towards the tree that was glowing with scintillating purplish bluish light. An old tribe opened the door of the tree “Here is your daughter! “
“Where is Mayura?”
“You mean the Peacock Deity?” replied the old Tribe with a smile

AYSHA LATHEEF

Aysha is from Aluva, Ernakulam, a bustling suburban town nestled on the banks of Periyar River. After completing her graduation in Agricultural Science, she is currently working as a Farm Officer in Mannuthy, Thrissur. She usually writes poems and short stories with 'love' as core theme. She is equally proficient both in English and Malayalam and has the experience of being an editor from her college days.

RADCLIFFE

The wild moon came up. Nothing was clear. He was just walking. No vibrations and there was no rye. He remembered that the bird that had flown away in the evening, terrified. He stared out over the fence, knowing his feet were sweating inside the boot, despite the cold outside. As usual, he stood looking at her arrive. Even then, the routine did not go wrong. She came running. Sweat was dripping down her forehead. He tried to wipe her sweat off with his palm, but she refused. They knew that those fences would always stand in the way of their love. "Laila...you still have fear on your face." He said. She again looked at him. "You soldiers do not know what fear is....we are different." She said. He smiled as he looked at her fingers moving with every word. He loved them and those endless wonders in her eyes... The depth of their love was as much as the silence between them. Knee-high bushes on both sides of the fence, occasional dark yellow flowers, and tall Poplar trees and flowering shrubs on the other side of the fence were the only witness to that deep love. There were no language barriers between them. And there was no any distinction between either India or Pakistan. She picked up a package from inside the shawl for him. It had *chapattis* and *spinach sabzi.* He looked into her eyes as she handed it to him across the fence. He sighed deeply. She was beginning to realize that there was a world beyond her home. He was the soldier who connected her to that world. They loved each other a lot, even though they were aware of the shortcomings. She loved his eyes and the unconditional love for his country. But she was afraid of the gunshots heard here and there every night. "I have a gun". He showed her the gun. "It is a semi-automatic Taurus pistol". He said. She felt nothing beyond the black

deadly object. “I am scared to death”. He shoved it inside the boot. “Do you have the courage to do that?” “For what…?” “To kill someone with this..?? To kill my brothers…” He moved closer to the fence…” I love you…Laila…I love you as much as each of our countries”. He saw her smile with both innocence and wisdom

ANIKA GULATI

Anika Gulati is a 12 year old dreamer, and an active student at Ryan International School Chandigarh.
She has won various medals in Mixed Martial Arts.
Writing is one of her hobbies and she loves penning down her thoughts in her diary.
She also likes cooking and baking.

THE TWO WITCHES

Once upon a time, there were two fast friends called Mantika and Avantika who studied in the same class. They were so close that they did everything together. They ate together, played together and shared secrets with each other. One day they decided to visit the City Museum but somehow they got very late in reaching there. Soon, it was time for the museum to close. The two girls decided amongst themselves to remain in the museum even after it's closed so that they could explore the place on their own. The girls, therefore, hid behind the huge antique shelf. And the guard, therefore, could not spot them. Now, the story goes that the Museum was haunted. The management and the staff knew that. It was a very well-kept secret. At night they would often hear weird sounds and thumping on the museum door. However, in the morning things went back to being normal. The girls were locked inside the museum and it was all dark. Avantika asked Mantika to turn on her phone's torch since her phone's battery was running low. Before Mantika could do that, they both felt a soft breeze touch their skin and in the dim light of the phone torch, they saw the utmost bizarre sight. The roof over the museum lifted a bit and started rotating clockwise. And then suddenly all the livestock in the Museum, lizards, rats, ants started matching in a row. A ladylike figure dressed in black was leading them. They went around the Museum as the girls watched all of this in horror. The troupe now reached the heavy museum door and started banging it. The guards obviously ignored these sounds. It was routine for them. The girls passed the night praying to God, whose existence they were previously skeptical about. In the morning, the doors were opened and the girls rushed out of the museum. They went straight to the police station and

related the string of events to them. The policemen were amused. They didn't believe any of it. The girls were sent back. For a few days, the girls talked about the witch in the museum but no one believed them. People thought the girls were strange for they talked about strange things. Some of those people also coined an appellation to denote the two friends who talked strangely. The appellation was: "Those two witches".

AMAL HASSAN

Amal Hassan is a student who has a love for creativity and enjoys experimenting with various arts. Being always a pro in arts, she was also a drama artist. When not writing, Amal enjoys exploring the outdoors with her friends.

NAIL POLISH

Raj once asked me with much excitement, "Seetha, what do you like most in this world?" Why you asking me this now? I asked back not knowing what he was so excited about. "You just tell me. I want to know about your every like and dislike." Raj was not so blank and so direct this time. "Nail polish" I give a very simple answer. "Nail polish? Is that so?" He asked. "My mom also likes nail polish a lot.

I have never even seen my mom without nail polish on her fingers. The colour of my mom's nails changes with each saree of hers on each night." I said somehow in a slightly nagging tone. "Seetha your nails are always white in colour right? I have never seen it as colourful or with nail polish." Raj asked. "I haven't put any nail polish in my life so far. My mom has not yet allowed me to put it on my nails. Every night I get rush to put nail polish with my mom. Then my mom fills an empty nail polish bottle with water and put it in my nails." I smiled and replied "Doesn't a mother want her daughter to be as beautiful as her mother?" I couldn't give him a correct answer for that.

But there were some words I was having in my mind that I couldn't express to him. Every night my mom applied different colour nail polish not because of her wish. Each colour was for different men. Mom is scared of me rushing to put on nail polish. She didn't give me any of those colours so that I would not be like her. But I still have those empty nail polish bottles filled with water in my hand.

Nail polish bottles that I kept in memory of my mother.

MOHIT SHARMA

Mohit Sharma is an author, poet, researcher, and social activist from Meerut who believes ideas are (slightly) more important than exposition. He is the founder of Freelance Talents, Kavya Comics (Poetry Comics), and Indian Comics Fandom. Mohit has a distinctively vivid background as his published works include anthologies, comics, articles, blogs, movies, novels, podcasts, non-fiction etc. He has contributed Hindi and English columns-articles for the local media, websites over the years. Alternate names - मोहित शर्मा ज़हन, Mohit Trendster, Education - MA Journalism & Mass Communication, MBA (Energy Finance).

HERD MORTALITY

There was once a herd of sheep grazing in a field near a cliff. They saw a group of dark figures heading toward them. One sheep cried, “Wolves!” The herd panicked, and being sheep, they ran in the opposite direction, toward the cliff. They reached the edge, stood there waiting for their inevitable demise. All of a sudden, the sheep heard a mighty roar in the distance. The dark figures retreated immediately. As they rejoiced, a Tiger strolled casually toward the herd. “You saved us?” asked the sheep. “No, I did not save you. It was the Holy Tiger who lives in the moon. "The sheep began dancing around, all the while praising the Holy Tiger. They begged the Tiger to escort them to a nearby field, he agreed. Next morning, the Tiger gathered the sheep together. “Last night, the Holy Tiger appeared to me in a dream. He saved your lives; in return, he demands a sacrifice. We must go back to the cliff upon which you were liberated and offer three of your lives,” The sheep were frightened but they were grateful to the Holy Tiger that they agreed. He led them to the cliff once more, and three sheep stepped forward. Tiger - “Do not be afraid, you will go to be with the Holy Tiger forever.” Tiger took the three sheep and led them to the edge of the cliff. The others watched while the Tiger began conducting the rite, preparing them for the sacrifice. As they watched, a hungry pack of hyenas advanced toward them. The sheep were so busy praising the Holy Tiger that they didn’t notice. They flanked the group, and gobbled up the sheep one by one. The others were oblivious to what was going on, and the hyenas continued until there were none left. Hyena Leader - “You were right. Sneaking in undetected proved to be much more fruitful than charging in and eating only the slowest. It was a great setup. How did you do it?” Tiger - “I

told them they had been saved by the ‘Holy Tiger’. They were so thankful that they would do anything I told them to do.” The pack broke into laughter at this, and the Tiger laughed heartily with them. “The oldest trick in the book. As we agreed, this entire domain is yours,” said the leader. “I hope we can do business again.”

VIVEK DUTTA MISHRA

Vivek is the author of the best-selling epic fiction The Accursed God. He has been working as a software technology enabler with various multinational technology giants for over twenty years. But his real passion lies in busting myths and glorifying Indian epics and history. With over three decades of study of Mahabharata, Ramayana and Indian history, he is a popular and acclaimed writer at social networks like Quora, podcast and other social networks.

He is reachable at
Web: http://vivek.vnc.in
Instagram: https://instagram.com/vivekduttamishra
Twitter: @vivekdmishra

THE MANUSCRIPT

I woke up. It was midnight. I could see the light coming from my study. I had it turned off before heading to the bed. Was it the light that woke me up or the voices coming from the other room? *Who could be in the room at this hour?*

"Ah, our friend is awake", said the man in the cream-coloured suit as I walked into my study. He was of ordinary height, ordinarily built and had a dusky complexion—to sum up, he was extraordinary.

"What are you doing in my study at midnight?" I asked. *Shouldn't I be asking him first—who the hell is he? Do I know him?*

"Are you sure it's midnight?" He asked; his smile never wavering.

Ah! Afternoon it is. I looked around, disbelieving.

"Look, Sir, this is where our friend is asking you, why you remained silent when they humiliated Draupadi?" He turned towards his older friend in a white suit — tall, well built with long white hair and beard.

"Get away from my manuscript!" I shouted, running and shoving it aside.

"He also asks why you sided with Duryodhana." The duo continued to ignore me, continuing their conversation. Was that a conversation? The older gentleman barely replied with a nod or a smile.

"That's my copyright!" I shouted.

"Ah! Are we your copyright?" The older guy's baritone resonated like something ancient. But it made no sense.

Who are these people? Why are they here?

"Because you called us."

"Did I? Are you some publishing agent?"

"Do I look like a publishing agent?" He countered, looking incredulous.

"No, Krishna! You very much look like yourself," the older gentleman replied, amused.

Now, the three of us were sitting by the side of a river Yamuna, watching the sunset. Krishna was back in his traditional yellow dhoti and his signature peacock-feathered crown. His partner, in his warrior attire and with his battle-scars, was hard not to recognize — Bhishma! The two certainly looked more comfortable in their traditional attire than the suit they were donning moments ago.

Bhishma thundered — "Who are you to fictionalize our lives? Why would you pull our strings like we are some puppets? Are we a figment of your imagination? Your copyright?"

Is this a dream?

Krishna whispered, smiling — "Of course it is a dream. But who says you are not answerable to questions asked in a dream?"

Flairs and Glairs, a platform by a student for the students. We are esteemed youth struggling to carve out our path for our future and we follow a basic mindset Since everyone is not born with all-round skills. Joining hands with people who are born to execute it with perfection is the best way to evolve. Self-Evolution is the need of the hour but, evolving as a community is what we strive for. The initiative as kickstarted by, Founder- Mr. Shubham Shah with the motive to utilize the skillset and talent of writing has now a team of 10+ people who are actively participating into newer forms of learning and discovering talents among youngsters. We Provide platform and services like Publishing opportunities, Open mics, Workshops, Hands-on training. Operating with Brand Name of Flairs and Glairs (Publication House), we offer the chance of elevating a passionate writer to an esteemed author With Brand name Teekhe Zasbaaat. We bring to you an opportunity to get accustomed with the Public Speaking and Presenting of Thoughts along with regular challenges to brush up your inking spirit. The newest initiative to extend our services we introduced in a new writing Platform- The Glittering Fables and Ink Over Tears.

We Choose to Fly Like A Falcon than to be

a Leg Pulling Crab.

www.ingramcontent.com/pod-product-compliance
Ingram Content Group UK Ltd.
Pitfield, Milton Keynes, MK11 3LW, UK
UKHW022004190726
13853UKWH00004B/1721